SOME OF IDAVILLE'S MOST
PROMINENT CITIZENS . . .

SMELLY NELLIE—She has the highest
paid nose in town. And she's only nine
years old!

BUGS MEANY—He's so mean he would
like to twist Encyclopedia's head
around so people could talk in front of
his face behind his back!

WILFORD WIGGINS—A high-school dropout with a million-dollar scheme to bilk
Idaville's kids out of their allowances!

BUSTER WILDE—The football star who
likes to practice every day by ramming
his head into tree trunks!

SUMNER FINKLEFOOTER—Who once
swallowed five nickels because his
father said he'd like to see some change
in him!

MEET EACH AND EVERY ONE OF
THEM AS
ENCYCLOPEDIA BROWN
TRACKS THEM DOWN!

HEY, KIDS!

Do you have a wacky story to tell about an animal, a fact, a crime, a sport? The funnier and wackier the better! But it must be *true*.

You can write about it, or enclose a clipping from your local newspaper, or send a note from your parents or teacher verifying the story. If it is included in an Encyclopedia Brown book, your name will appear in the book.

Send your wacky true story (along with your name and address) to: Encyclopedia Brown, c/o Bantam Books, 666 Fifth Avenue, New York 10103.

AMERICA'S SHERLOCK HOLMES IN SNEAKERS · No. 8

ENCYCLOPEDIA BROWN
Tracks Them Down
Donald J. Sobol

Illustrated by Leonard Shortall

A BANTAM SKYLARK BOOK

This low-priced Bantam Book
has been completely reset in a type face
designed for easy reading, and was printed
from new plates. It contains the complete
text of the original hard-cover edition.
NOT ONE WORD HAS BEEN OMITTED.

RL 3, IL 3+

ENCYCLOPEDIA BROWN TRACKS THEM DOWN

A Bantam Book / published by arrangement with
Thomas Nelson Inc.

PRINTING HISTORY

Thomas Nelson edition published October 1971
A Junior Literary Guild Selection 1978
A Selection of Book-of-the-Month Club, Meridith Corporation,
Xerox Education Publications and Archway.

Bantam Skylark edition / February 1981
2nd printing . . . . July 1981

ISBN 0-553-15139-8

Published simultaneously in the United States and Canada

Bantam Books are published by Bantam Books, Inc. Its trademark, consisting of the words ''Bantam Books'' and the por-
trayal of a bantam, is Registered in U.S. Patent and Trademark
Office and in other countries. Marca Registrada. Bantam
Books, Inc., 666 Fifth Avenue, New York, New York 10103.

PRINTED IN THE UNITED STATES OF AMERICA

11 10 9 8 7 6 5 4 3

BOOK DESIGNED BY MIERRE

*For
Parry
and
Rae Larsen*

Contents

Encyclopedia Brown
Tracks Them Down

The Case
of the
Champion Skier

Dinner at the Browns' red brick house in Idaville was not like dinner in other homes.

The Browns not only broke bread together. They broke crimes together.

Mr. Brown was chief of police. People everywhere thought that he was the brains behind Idaville's wonderful record of law and order.

Nobody could have guessed the truth. Behind Chief Brown's success was his only child—ten-year-old Encyclopedia.

Chief Brown brought home his hardest cases. Encyclopedia solved them while eating dinner. Since he had begun secretly helping his father, no crook had escaped arrest, and no child had got away with ducking the law.

Chief Brown would have liked to pin a medal on Encyclopedia every time his son solved a case. But what good would it do?

Who would believe that the real mastermind behind Idaville's crime cleanup was a fifth grader?

Besides, Encyclopedia couldn't have stood up under all the medals without getting flat feet.

So Chief Brown said nothing.

Encyclopedia never let slip a word about the help he gave his father. He did not want to seem different from other boys.

However, there was nothing he could do about his nickname.

Only his parents and teachers called him by his right name, Leroy. Everyone else called him Encyclopedia.

An encyclopedia is a book or set of

books full of facts from A to Z—like Encyclopedia's brain. He had done more reading than just about anybody in town. His pals said that when he turned a cartwheel, his head sounded like a bookcase falling over.

But one evening Chief Brown brought home a case Encyclopedia couldn't solve during dinner.

Chief Brown explained why. "We don't have any facts," he said.

Mrs. Brown was relieved. "No wonder Leroy can't help you," she said. "What kind of crime is it, dear?"

"Kidnapping," answered Chief Brown. "One of our ambassadors in Latin America has been kidnapped. That's all I've been told. The State Department wants me to fly down and see what I can do."

"It sounds like a top-secret case," said Encyclopedia. "Boy, I wish I could go along!"

"You can," said his father. "The State Department wants my visit to look like a family holiday. So all three of us are going."

Encyclopedia Brown

The next morning Encyclopedia had his first view of Idaville from the sky.

He couldn't tell the houses of the rich families from those of the poor families, the churches from the synagogues, or the delicatessens from the banks.

Before he had had time to pick out his own house, the jet was flying over the Gulf of Mexico. He opened his book, *Vertebrate Paleontology*. As he reached the last chapter, the jet put down with a light bump.

At the airport the Browns were met by a man in a dark suit. He said he was a chauffeur from the hotel. He loaded their bags into the back of a green car.

As he started the engine, he introduced himself again. He was really Mr. Rico, a police officer.

"The kidnapped man is Mr. Ware, your ambassador here," he said. "We are going to his home now."

On the way, Mr. Rico told Chief Brown all the facts that were known about the case.

Mr. Ware had been kidnapped two

At the airport the Browns were met by a man in a dark suit.

days earlier. He had been driving to a hotel in the mountains for a week of skiing. His empty car had been found in the snow two miles below the hotel.

"Mr. Ware is a champion water skier," said Mr. Rico. "But he had never skied on snow. He wanted to learn."

"Had he ever been to the hotel in the mountains before?" asked Chief Brown.

"No," replied Mr. Rico. "He told no one where he was going except his wife. In fact, he got a room at the hotel under a different name."

"Why did he want to do that?" inquired Mrs. Brown.

"For safety's sake," replied Mr. Rico. "Foreign service has become dangerous here. People who don't like the government have taken to kidnapping foreign officials."

"How much money are the kidnappers asking for Mr. Ware's return?" said Chief Brown.

"The kidnappers never want money," answered Mr. Rico. "They want their friends freed from prison. For Mr. Ware, they are demanding the freedom of forty men being held in prison for crimes against the government."

"How awful!" exclaimed Mrs. Brown. "Kidnapping an innocent man to win freedom for criminals!"

Mr. Rico continued. "The night Mr. Ware disappeared, he gave a birthday party for himself. He was forty-five. He invited six friends. Each brought a gift. They came at eight o'clock and found food, servants, and a note from Mr. Ware. The note said he'd had to leave the city early and for everyone to enjoy the party without him."

"Was there a reason for his missing his own party?" inquired Chief Brown.

"There was a weather report of a snowstorm due that night," said Mr. Rico. "He must have figured that if he stayed for the party, he'd find the mountain roads to the hotel snowbound. So he left the city before the storm."

Mr. Rico stopped the car in front of the ambassador's large house. He unlocked the front door.

On the sofa in the living room were the six birthday gifts.

"I opened them," said Mr. Rico. "I thought there might be a clue among them, but there wasn't."

Encyclopedia and his father looked over the gifts. Each gift had a card bearing the name of the guest who had brought it to Mr. Ware's party.

They were a spear gun from Bill Watson, a can of ski wax from Harry Smith, a face mask from Dan Perske, an air tank from Kurt Haper, a pair of water skis from Marty Benton, and a rubber diving suit from Ed Furgis.

Mr. Rico said, "Mrs. Ware is certain that her husband told no one about the trip to the mountains but herself."

"Mr. Ware must be a proud man," said Chief Brown. "He doesn't want to be seen doing anything until he can do it well."

"Yes," agreed Mr. Rico. "He is a champion water skier. But he didn't want anyone to see him learning to ski on snow and perhaps looking silly. So he kept his trip a secret."

"He *must* have told someone besides his wife," said Chief Brown. "And that someone worked with the kidnappers."

Mr. Rico nodded. "But whom did Mr. Ware tell?"

Chief Brown looked at Encyclopedia.

Encyclopedia whispered, "He told ..."

WHOM?

(Turn to page 103 for the solution to The Case of the Champion Skier.)

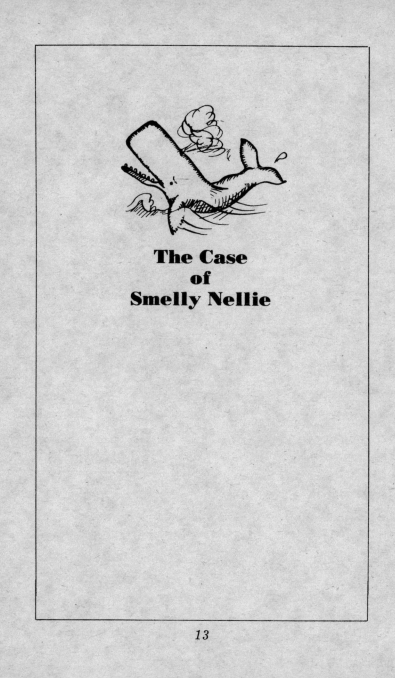

The Case
of
Smelly Nellie

Encyclopedia helped his father solve mysteries at the dinner table all year around. In the summer, he helped the children of the neighborhood as well.

When school let out, he opened his own detective agency in the garage. Every morning he hung out his sign:

BROWN DETECTIVE AGENCY
13 Rover Avenue
Leroy Brown, President
No case too small
25¢ per day
plus expenses

One day Smelly Nellie came into the garage. She was only nine years old. Yet she already had earned the money for her college education.

She had done it with her nose alone.

When she was eight, she had saved the city hall from being blown to kingdom come. She had sniffed out a leak in the gas line running into the building just as Mr. Barnes, the mayor, was about to light a cigar nearby.

As a reward, the city council had set aside money to pay her way through the college of her choice.

After that, no one called her by her real name, Nelita Theodora Shortridge. Everyone called her Smelly Nellie for short.

Her nose didn't stop at sniffing gas leaks. It could smell a marshmallow roast—or anything else—three blocks away, rain or shine.

When she came into the Brown Detective Agency, however, she wasn't using her nose. She was holding it.

"Ambergris," she gagged.

Encyclopedia had read about ambergris. It is thrown up by sick whales. It is found floating in southern waters and is used in making perfume.

"Don't just sit there," piped Smelly Nellie. "Bring a bottle of oil of peppermint!"

Encyclopedia jumped to it. Within twenty seconds he was shoving an open bottle under Smelly Nellie's wonderful nose. She breathed deeply.

"Thanks," she sighed. "It's the only thing to clear the passages."

"What snarled the sneezer?" asked Encyclopedia.

"Did you ever stand close to ambergris?" asked Smelly Nellie. "It's worse than being scorekeeper at a skunk fight."

She laid twenty-five cents on the gas can beside Encyclopedia.

"I want you to get back my ambergris," she said. "Bugs Meany stole it!"

"Give Bugs a free hand, and he'll stick it right into your pocket," said Encyclopedia.

Bugs Meany was the leader of a gang

of tough older boys. Encyclopedia had often been hired to stop their stealing and cheating.

"Let's go speak with Bugs," said Encyclopedia.

The two children took the Number 7 bus. During the ride, Smelly Nellie told her story.

She had found the ambergris washed up on the beach at Lighthouse Point that morning while she was smelling for clams.

"Bugs Meany and his Tigers were skin diving offshore," she said. "I asked them to help me get the stuff home."

The Tigers had laughed and told her to go chase herself. So Smelly Nellie had to tell them the truth. A company in New York City was paying five dollars an ounce for ambergris.

"I found a lump that must weigh fifty pounds," she said.

Encyclopedia whistled and did some figuring: sixteen times fifty times five— four thousand dollars!

"That's enough money to buy a car," he said.

"Bugs Meany thought the same," said Smelly Nellie. "When he heard what ambergris is worth, he asked me if I thought he'd look good in a sports car. Then he told me to scram."

The bus halted at the last stop, and the children got off. They walked along the beach toward Lighthouse Point.

After about a mile, Smelly Nellie gave a cry and pinched her nose. Encyclopedia took the warning and did likewise.

Another few steps brought them around a bend. They saw the lighthouse and the Tigers.

The Tigers had done no more than beach their boat. They were lying on their backs, holding their noses and groaning.

The lump of ambergris was still on the wet sand at the high-tide line. It looked like a ball of dark-gray wax.

"The Tigers haven't got away with the stuff yet," said Smelly Nellie gleefully. "The smell flattened 'em!"

Bugs Meany was the first to see Smelly Nellie and the boy detective. He shouted the alarm and sat up weakly.

"Beat it," he growled at Encyclopedia.

The Tigers were lying on their backs, holding their
noses and moaning.

"Or I'll yank your tongue so hard your ears will roll up like window shades."

Encyclopedia was used to Bugs's greeting. "The ambergris belongs to Smelly Nellie," he said. "She found the lump this morning."

"Me and my Tigers found the lump on the bottom of the ocean while we were skin´diving," retorted Bugs.

"Then how did it get on the beach?" demanded Encyclopedia.

"We rolled it under the water," replied Bugs Meany. "Then we waited for the tide to go out so we could lift it into the boat."

"Y-you horse's neck!" cried Smelly Nellie. "You're lying!"

"And I can prove it," added Encyclopedia.

HOW?

(Turn to page 104 for the solution to The Case of Smelly Nellie.)

The Case
of the
Flying Submarine

The only thing Bugs Meany wanted for Christmas was a chance to get even with Encyclopedia.

Bugs hated being outsmarted by the boy detective. He longed to screw Encyclopedia's head around so people would talk in front of his face behind his back.

But every time Bugs got such ideas, he remembered Sally Kimball, Encyclopedia's junior partner. Sally was the prettiest girl in the fifth grade and the best athlete.

She was also the only one—boy or

girl—under twelve whom Bugs feared. Every time he had mixed with her, she had left him on the ground to cool.

Because of Sally, Bugs never tried to push Encyclopedia around. He never stopped trying to gain revenge, however.

"We'd better watch out for Bugs," warned Sally. "He's like a man fixing a ten-foot clock. He's always trying to get the upper hand."

The detectives were biking into town to look over the new line of cheese cakes at the Tasty Delicatessen. They had taken a shortcut, which was a mistake. The dirt path was slippery with mud after a two-day rain.

The path led near Mr. Sweeny's Auto Body Shop. Behind the shop stood the old tool shed which Bugs and his Tigers used for a clubhouse.

As the clubhouse came into view, a helicopter roared overhead. Encyclopedia glanced up and saw a tiny gray submarine flying through the air. It crashed into the thick woods west of the clubhouse.

Encyclopedia and Sally jumped off their bikes. They dashed for the woods as

Bugs Meany and two of his Tigers, Dutch Kuller and Jess Rae, came racing out of the clubhouse.

They all drew up at the muddy edge of a hollow. At the bottom rested the submarine. It was smashed, a total loss.

"Man, oh, man!" cried Bugs. "It's an enemy bomb!"

"It's a mini-sub, you baboon," corrected Sally.

"Who ever heard of a sub that small and round?" jeered Bugs. "It's some kind of long-range bomb, that's what it is, sent by a certain country to blast us Tigers!"

Bugs raved on about how "a certain country" was out to get every real American, like his Tigers. Encyclopedia looked up at the sky. The helicopter had flown away. There was no place for it to land near the woods.

Sally started down the muddy slope toward the sub.

"Stay back!" hollered Bugs. "That thing can go off any second!"

He winked at Dutch and Jess. Then he stuck out his foot, tripping Sally. She rolled down the slope.

Bugs stuck out his foot, tripping Sally.

"It's an enemy spaceship," sang Bugs. "Those purple guys from Mars carry freeze guns. They'll turn you into an ice-cream pie, *rat-tat-tat*."

"Darn you, Bugs Meany," gasped Sally, wiping mud from her eyes.

Bugs stepped toward Encyclopedia. "Us Tigers will stand guard till the FBI arrives," he said. "You and Miss Mud Bath can clear out—now!"

"And give you a chance to steal everything inside the sub?" asked Encyclopedia. "Not on your life."

"Okay, Mr. Foxy Nose," snarled Bugs. He lifted his fists. "You've been asking for this all summer. Nobody's around, so—"

"Don't you dare!" shouted Sally.

"Stay out of it," warned Bugs. "I don't want to dirty my hands on you." He made a great show of flicking a speck of mud from his otherwise clean pants.

Jess strutted to where Sally was struggling up the slope from the submarine. "Me and Dutch will handle the dame," he boasted.

He bent to push Sally. All at once he was sliding in the mud.

Sally had grabbed his arm and yanked. Before Jess knew what was coming next, she had hit him in the stomach. The one punch tamed all three Tigers.

Jess lay in the mud making noises like a falling roof. Bugs and Dutch looked as if the roof had fallen on them.

"J-Jess!" spluttered Dutch. "C-can you breathe?"

Jess's reply was lost in the scream of police sirens. In a few minutes six officers, led by Chief Brown, had circled the sub.

Encyclopedia learned from his father what was going on. The sub had been on its way to the Naval Base for tests.

"When it fell from the sling, the pilot radioed police headquarters," said Chief Brown. "It's a secret weapon. We must guard it till the Navy people can take over."

"You got here just in time, Chief," said Bugs. "In another hour, the sub would have been stripped clean."

"How's that?" said Chief Brown.

"I sure hate to tell you this," said Bugs. "Your son and Sally tried to break into the sub and steal what's inside."

"We did nothing of the sort," protested Encyclopedia.

"We aren't asking for medals, but I'll tell you that us Tigers did our best to stop them without using force," said Bugs.

"Liar!" cried Sally. "If you had laid a hand on me, I'd have given you what Jess got."

"You talk mighty big," said Bugs. "You know Tigers don't fight girls."

"Your son told Sally to open the sub," put in Jess. "Bugs attempted to talk her out of it. So she tripped him. After he went down, I tried to tell her she was doing wrong, but she's a wildcat. She tripped me, too."

"She was trying to open the sub when you arrived, Chief," added Bugs.

Chief Brown looked concerned. "This is serious, Leroy. It's your word against theirs."

"Don't take my word, Dad," said Encyclopedia. "Look at—"

LOOK AT WHAT?

*(Turn to page 105 for the solution to
The Case of the Flying Submarine.)*

31

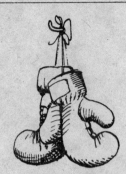

The Case
of the
Boy Boxers

Sunday afternoon, Encyclopedia was reading the newspaper when the telephone rang.

The caller was Elmer Otis. He talked so fast that Encyclopedia had to run in place to keep up.

"Elmer," said the boy detective. *"Elmer!* Calm down."

"I'm calm as a clam," shot back Elmer. "Get the police! Get your father!"

"What's the trouble?" asked Encyclopedia.

"I'm at the Youth Center," said Elmer. "Somebody just robbed the cash box in the office."

The cash in the office of the Youth Center never amounted to more than three dollars. The money was kept in a cigar box. It was used to make change for the candy and soda machines.

"This isn't exactly a case for the police," said Encyclopedia.

"It's a case for someone," replied Elmer. "You'd better get over here while the trail is hot."

Hot trails always warmed Encyclopedia's blood. He climbed on his bike and rode to the Youth Center.

He was surprised to find Sally sitting outside.

"Boys," she muttered in disgust.

"What's the matter with boys?" demanded Encyclopedia.

"They do more talking than punching," answered Sally.

She explained. Although the Youth Center was usually closed on Sundays, Elmer and two pals, Pete and Oscar, had been allowed to use it. They were training for the junior boxing championships next week.

"They wanted me to lace on their gloves and act as referee," said Sally. "But . . . phew! They're afraid to get hit. I grew sick of watching them. So I came outside till they'd need me to take off their gloves."

"They're saving themselves for the tournament, I'm sure," said Encyclopedia in defense of his sex. Then he told Sally about Elmer's telephone call and the stolen money.

"Did you see anyone leave the building while you were sitting out front?" he asked.

"No, the building is empty except for those three cream puffs," said Sally.

She frowned and suddenly clapped her hands. "Wait! Jim Hill . . . I saw him come from behind the building. He walked away in a terrible hurry."

"Jim could have sneaked in and out by the back door," observed Encyclopedia. "He may be the thief."

"Not Jim," objected Sally. "He wasn't even smart enough to become a Tiger.

Bugs Meany says he stands in front of a mirror with his eyes closed to see how he looks when he's asleep."

"Maybe Jim had help," murmured Encyclopedia.

The two detectives went inside. Elmer, Pete, and Oscar were in the gym. They wore boxing gloves.

Elmer was shadowboxing in a corner. Pete and Oscar were sparring in perfect safety. Neither came within a mile of landing a punch.

"When I hit you on the nose, you'll smell leather for a week," promised Oscar without moving closer.

"Yeah? Well, if I hang one on your chin, your socks will fly off," retorted Pete, keeping his distance.

"The windbags," thought Encyclopedia. "Sally could deck them both in half a round."

Elmer stopped shadowboxing and came over to Encyclopedia.

"The theft must have happened a few minutes after Sally went outside," he said. "The three of us were in the gym. We heard a crash in the back of the building."

Elmer, Pete, and Oscar were in the gym. They wore
boxing gloves.

"Did you all go to see what it was?" asked Encyclopedia.

"Yes—it was a lamp," said Elmer. "I'll show you."

The children walked down the hall to the back of the building, turned right, and entered the office.

The cigar box, in which the money was kept, lay on the desk, empty. A broken lamp was on the floor.

"We left everything as you see it," said Elmer.

Encyclopedia opened the large office closet. Next, he walked out of the office and tried the back door. It opened from the inside. It was locked, however, to anyone on the outside.

"Did any of you three leave the gym by himself?" asked Encyclopedia.

"We all did at one time or another," said Elmer. "We went for a drink of water."

The water fountain was across the hall from the back door. Encyclopedia stepped on the foot pedal and took a drink.

"The office, the back door, and the water fountain can't be seen from the gym," he said thoughtfully. "And the office can't be seen from the water fountain or the back door."

"Is that a clue?" asked Elmer.

"Of course!" exclaimed Sally. "Any one of you could have gone for a drink, opened the back door, and let in the thief without being seen."

"But the thief couldn't have escaped without our seeing him," protested Elmer. "When we heard the crash, Oscar, Pete, and I rushed to the office."

"And while Elmer telephoned you for help, Pete and I were at the water fountain," said Oscar. "The thief couldn't have slipped past us."

"The thief didn't," said Encyclopedia. "When he knocked over the lamp he hid in the closet. Not until you three had looked around the office and returned to the gym did he run out the back door."

"Do you really believe one of us helped the thief?" asked Elmer angrily.

"The other way around," said Encyclopedia. "The thief helped one of you."

WHOM DID ENCYCLOPEDIA SUSPECT?

(Turn to page 106 for the solution to The Case of the Boy Boxers.)

The Case
of the
Model Universe

Encyclopedia was sweeping the garage after dinner when he saw Hugo Dipman walk into a lamp post.

"Hugo!" called Encyclopedia. "Are you all right?"

"I—I'm okay," gasped Hugo. He staggered around on the sidewalk as if he didn't know whether he was on his head or his heels. "I was looking up at the stars and counting my money."

"Counting . . . ?" said Encyclopedia. "Hey, you're hurt worse than you think."

"I may be walking around like a left-footed pony, but I know what I'm talking about," insisted Hugo. "I'm going to make money out of the stars. Wilford Wiggins says so."

Wilford Wiggins was a high school dropout. He kept Encyclopedia busy stopping his get-rich-quick deals from cheating the children of the neighborhood.

"You can't trust Wilford," warned Encyclopedia. "He'd rather cheat than eat. Why, he'd pin a badge on a frankfurter and sell it as a police dog."

"I know Wilford is as crooked as a corkscrew," said Hugo. "But this time it's different. He's really got a plan to make all us little kids millionaires."

"What's the plan?" asked Encyclopedia.

"Wilford says he'll make any kid five dollars for every star that can be seen with the naked eye," said Hugo. "Wilford is holding a meeting at two o'clock tomorrow in South Park to explain his idea."

"Wilford forgot to tell me about the meeting," mused Encyclopedia.

"He's not exactly wild about you," pointed out Hugo. "You've put him down so often he's beginning to squeak like a drawbridge."

"Trouble is, he always comes back up," said Encyclopedia. "I think I'd better go along with you tomorrow."

After lunch the next day, Encyclopedia left Sally in charge of the detective agency. He went with Hugo to South Park.

"We're just in time," said Hugo.

Wilford Wiggins was standing close to the statue of Abraham Lincoln.

"Boy, is he trying to look wise and honest," murmured Encyclopedia. "The phony! I wouldn't believe him even if he swore he was lying."

A large crowd of children had gathered in front of Wilford. He raised his hands and called for quiet.

"Step right up, boys and girls," he began. "I'm going to tell you how you can get so rich and important you'll need two desks—one for each foot!"

"Your jokes get worse," complained Benny Breslin.

"Okay, I'm no clown," said Wilford.

A large crowd of children had gathered in front of Wilford.

"I'm a square shooter. I'm going to let you in on the biggest secret deal of your lives."

In the back of the crowd someone started clapping. Wilford believed he was being applauded and bowed.

"Aw, you big dummy. I was slapping my head to keep awake," shouted Bugs Meany. He pushed to the front. "Tell us your money-making idea and cut out the chin music."

"You can't wait, eh, kid?" said Wilford. "Greed, it's wonderful! Everyone wants easy money. Well, your friend and neighbor Wilford Wiggins is going to get it for you—with this!"

He reached into his pocket. The children pressed forward.

"Here it is!" cried Wilford. "Here is the money-making wonder!"

The children stared.

"What is it, you ask?" Wilford went on. "I'll tell you. It's a half-inch model of the earth!"

He passed the tiny ball among the children.

Then he continued: "My partner, Professor Wolfgang Schmidt of Germany, is building a model of the universe. We'll show it all over America."

"Making a model universe will cost a lot, won't it?" said Desmond Durand.

"You've got to spend money to make money," replied Wilford. "Professor Schmidt is trying to raise a million dollars. He'll need to manufacture thousands of stars and planets and moons and what not. Every child will want to see this exhibit! Every man and woman!"

The model of the earth was passed from hand to hand. At last it reached Hugo. "Sure looks good," he said.

"You can see with your own eyes that I'm not trying to trick you," said Wilford. "You can buy a share—each and every one of you—in this greatest show in history."

"How much is a share?" demanded Bugs, still doubtful but giving way to the call of easy money.

"Five dollars," replied Wilford. "In two years your measly five dollars will have grown into millions!"

The thrill of those millions swept through the crowd of children. More people would come to see the model universe than watched football!

"We could put the exhibit in the Astrodome!" said Carl Betts.

The suggestion started a storm of excitement. The children argued about where to put the model universe on exhibit. The Yankee Stadium! The Rose Bowl!

Lucy Fibbs had the biggest idea.

"Put it in the Grand Canyon!" she shrieked.

Nobody could top that—except Encyclopedia.

"Put it in the trash can," he said.

Instantly there was silence. All heads turned toward the boy detective.

"Save your money," he said. "You'll never see it again if you give it to Wilford."

WHY NOT?

*(Turn to page 107 for the solution to
The Case of the Model Universe.)*

The Case
of the
Flower Can

Stella Boswell ran into the Brown Detective Agency.

"A big boy just tried to rob me!" she cried.

"Of what?" asked Encyclopedia.

"These!" She held up a rusty can filled with wild flowers.

Encyclopedia gazed at the flowers. It was hard to think of anything less worth stealing, except maybe a stomachache.

"I want you to catch the thief," said Stella. "He's dangerous."

She put a coin on the gasoline can beside Encyclopedia. It didn't clink like a quarter. It clunked.

"I'm sorry, but it's the only money I have," she said. "Is it worth twenty-five cents?"

Encyclopedia picked up the coin. He turned three shades of pink.

"This is an 1861 Confederate silver half-dollar!" he exclaimed. "It's worth about five thousand dollars! Where did you get it?"

"Five thous——*ahhhh*," answered Stella. She stopped breathing, though her mouth was open wide enough to air out her toes. "Five—*ahhhh*."

Finally she swallowed hard and gasped out, "The big boy dropped it." Then she told what had happened.

She was returning from picking wild flowers when a boy of about eighteen ran by. The paper bag in his hand knocked against her shoulder and broke open.

"Coins fell all over the sidewalk," said Stella. "He picked them up and grabbed for my flower can. But a car drove up the street, and he ran away."

"Coins fell all over the sidewalk," said Stella.

"That's when you discovered the half-dollar had fallen into the flower can?" asked Encyclopedia.

"Yes, and I'm beginning to understand," said Stella with a sigh. "He wanted the coin and not my beautiful flowers."

"Would you know the boy if you saw him again?"

Stella shook her head. "Everything happened so quickly."

Encyclopedia's brain was going fast. The boy must have stolen the coins. Otherwise, he wouldn't have been scared off by a passing car.

He would be hanging around the neighborhood, waiting for another chance at Stella. . . .

Encyclopedia pushed her into the house and locked the doors. "Can you bake?" he inquired.

"Only sugar cookies," she replied. "They'll simply melt in your mouth."

"Great," said Encyclopedia and hurried to telephone police headquarters.

He wasn't surprised to learn that the theft of a rare coin collection had just been reported. He told his father about Stella and the Confederate half-dollar.

"I think I can trap the thief," said the boy detective.

Chief Brown listened to his son's plan. "It might work," he said. "I'll send Officer Hall and Policewoman Taylor to help you."

After giving the police officers half an hour to get into place, the two children started for Stella's house. Stella carried the flower can. Encyclopedia carried his own coin collection.

"I can feel someone watching us," whispered Stella.

"It's Officer Hall," said Encyclopedia. "He's across the street selling tickets to the policeman's ball door to door. The thief won't bother us while he's on the block."

When they entered Stella's house, they found Policewoman Taylor dressed as a maid.

Encyclopedia swiftly set the stage for the arrival of the thief.

He spread his coins on the kitchen table. The flower can with the wild flowers and the Confederate half-dollar he put behind the electric mixer, where it could not be easily seen.

Stella meanwhile got out what she needed to bake sugar cookies—butter, an egg, a bottle of vanilla, a can of baking powder, matching cans of sugar and flour, a teaspoon, a measuring cup, and a rolling pin.

"Officer Hall turned down Worth Street," said Policewoman Taylor from the window. "He just disappeared around the corner."

"We can expect our thief any minute," said Encyclopedia.

Five minutes later Policewoman Taylor answered the doorbell. She led a nervous boy of eighteen into the kitchen.

"Hi," he said. "My name is Bret. I'm selling magazines to work my way through college."

"I'm a great reader," said Stella. "What magazines are you selling?"

Bret took out a large folder showing many magazines.

"I can't look right now," said Stella. "Ooops!"

She had nearly knocked over the can of flour reaching for the butter.

"Would you hold the flour for me a second?" she asked.

"Sure," said Bret. He took the flour and glanced at the table, where Encyclopedia was rattling his coins noisily.

"Are you interested in coins?" asked the boy detective.

"It's sort of a hobby of mine," replied Bret.

"I found a funny coin this morning," said Stella.

"I'd like to see it," said Bret.

"I hid it in the flower can," said Stella, wiping her hands on her apron.

Bret walked around the kitchen till he spied the can of wild flowers sticking up behind the electric mixer. His eyes lit up as he seized it.

He was so busy digging out the Confederate half-dollar that he didn't notice Encyclopedia signal Policewoman Taylor.

Before Bret knew what was happening, the policewoman had snapped handcuffs on him.

HOW DID BRET
GIVE HIMSELF AWAY?

(Turn to page 108 for the solution to The Case of the Flower Can.)

The Case
of the
Half-White Horse

"I know that look," said Mrs. Brown across the dinner table. "You've solved an important case."

Chief Brown set down his soup spoon and grinned.

"Do you remember the Fairchild jewelry robbery?" he asked. "It happened last week in Glenn City."

"The stolen pieces of jewelry had little resale value," said Mrs. Brown. "But they had been in Mr. Fairchild's family for years. He was very upset by the robbery."

"That's right," said Chief Brown. "Mr.

65

Fairchild was afraid the thief would throw away the jewels when he discovered they were all nearly worthless. So Mr. Fairchild offered a five-thousand-dollar reward for their return, with no questions asked."

"Gosh, Dad," said Encyclopedia. "The thief took an awful chance returning the jewelry, even for five thousand dollars."

"The thief didn't return them," corrected Chief Brown. "Earle Coughlin spied the thief on the seaway riding path. Earle will get the reward."

"Who is the thief?" asked Mrs. Brown.

"Sol Schwartz," answered Chief Brown. "I had to arrest him."

Encyclopedia was shocked. Sol ran the Idaville Riding Academy and gave horseback-riding lessons. He was a big, friendly man.

Encyclopedia shook his head. "I can't believe Sol is a thief."

"We found some of the stolen jewelry—a set of cuff links—in his bedroom," said Chief Brown. "I'm sorry . . . I feel the same way about Sol as you do."

"Well, if you feel Sol is such a fine

man, why did you arrest him?" asked Mrs. Brown.

"The cuff links are enough evidence," replied Chief Brown. "And there is the witness, Earle Coughlin."

"Just what did Earle Coughlin say he saw?" demanded Mrs. Brown.

Chief Brown unbuttoned his breast pocket. He took out a notebook. Then he read what Earle Coughlin had told him.

"Yesterday I was out in my boat fishing. I had anchored a few hundred yards offshore. I noticed a horse and rider moving along the seaway riding path."

Chief Brown looked up and said, "The seaway riding path is only about six feet wide. It runs by the sea midway up a cliff of about a hundred feet." Then he read on.

"I was amazed to see the rider stop. I got out my field glasses. The horse was white and black, with a large bell-shaped black mark on the shoulder.

"The rider dismounted with his back to me, and so I couldn't be sure of his face then. But he had 'Idaville Riding Academy' sewn across the back of his shirt.

"The horse was white and black, with a large bell-shaped black mark on the shoulder."

"He went into a small opening in the cliff. When he came out, I could see it was Sol Schwartz. He mounted and rode off.

"I docked my boat, and being curious went into the cave. I found a sack filled with jewelry hidden under a rock. I reported what I had found immediately to the police."

"I checked the cave," said Chief Brown. "The jewelry in the sack matched the list of pieces stolen from Mr. Fairchild, except that a set of cuff links was missing. I got a warrant to search Sol Schwartz's home. The cuff links were in a dresser drawer in his bedroom."

"Did Sol confess?" asked Mrs. Brown.

"No," answered Chief Brown. "He said he'd never seen the cuff links before."

Encyclopedia sat in glum silence. Sol always wore a shirt with "Idaville Riding Academy" sewn on the back. Worse, the white-and-black horse with the bell-shaped mark on the shoulder was Half-and-Half. Only Sol rode him.

Half-and-Half was twenty-three, old for a horse. As the years had passed, the black spots had faded from his left side, leaving him entirely white there. But the side which Earle Coughlin had seen, the right side, remained spotted black and white.

Twice a week Sol took old Half-and-Half out for a ride along the seaway path and returned to the academy by the inland path through the woods.

"Sol admitted riding the horse on the seaway path when Earle Coughlin claims to have seen him," said Chief Brown. "But Sol says he never dismounted. He insists he had nothing to do with the jewelry robbery, either."

"Earle Coughlin could have put the jewels in the little cave himself," pointed out Mrs. Brown. "He could also have sneaked into Sol's bedroom, planted the cuff links in the drawer, and reported everything to you."

"Do you think he's trying to frame Sol?" asked Chief Brown.

"If Earle Coughlin is the real thief, he certainly would put the blame on someone else. Then he could collect the five-thousand-dollar reward," said Mrs. Brown.

"I've thought of that," said Chief Brown. "But Sol has no alibi for the time the jewelry was stolen from Mr. Fairchild. Sol says he was out riding when the robbery took place. Unfortunately, nobody saw him."

"Sol has got to be innocent," insisted Encyclopedia. "Something is wrong with Earle Coughlin's story."

The boy detective closed his eyes. He always closed his eyes when he did his hardest thinking.

"If Sol only had a witness besides Earle Coughlin," said Mrs. Brown.

Encyclopedia gave a start.

"That's it, Mom!" he exclaimed. "Sol does have another witness—old Half-and-Half!"

WHAT DID ENCYCLOPEDIA MEAN?

(Turn to page 109 for the solution to The Case of the Half-White Horse.)

The Case
of the
Apple Cider

Buster Wilde was the star of the West Side Midgets, Idaville's Peewee League football champions.

During the off-season, Buster carried his football helmet everywhere he went. Whenever he felt like it, he toughened up his skull. He put on the helmet and charged the nearest tree headfirst.

On the day he came into the Brown Detective Agency, however, he wasn't carrying his helmet. He was carrying a bird.

"Look what I found," he said. He laid the bird on the desk in front of Encyclopedia.

"It's a cedar waxwing," said Encyclopedia. "They fly through Idaville on their way north every summer. What about it?"

"This," said Buster and gave the bird a gentle poke. "Watch."

The bird took two steps and fell on its face.

"It's hurt, poor thing!" cried Sally.

"Naw," said Buster. "It's drunk."

Encyclopedia put his nose close to the bird's beak and sniffed.

"You've got a point," he gasped in disbelief. "It smells like a beer garden."

Buster explained that he had found the bird on the way to visit his grandmother.

"I saw this big oak tree," he said. "Since my grandmother doesn't like me to play football, I didn't bring my helmet. I decided to have a go at the tree anyway."

"*Bareheaded?*" exclaimed Sally.

"Yep," answered Buster. "I've always wondered how tough my head really is."

He had found out. When he awakened, the tree was still standing. But birds were falling off the branches.

"At first," said Buster, "I figured I was still dizzy. I wasn't. The birds were. They were so cock-eyed drunk they couldn't see through a ladder."

"That *I* want to see," said Encyclopedia.

Sally placed the tipsy bird in the sun to recover. Then the three children biked to the scene of the mystery.

Buster pointed to a large yard full of trees and berry bushes behind a white house. "See for yourself," he said.

Encyclopedia beheld dozens of birds, most of them cedar waxwings. Some were falling off branches. A few were flopping around as if lost in a fog. The rest were so high they couldn't even leave the ground.

The boy detective moved carefully among the birds and the berry bushes. Strangely, there were no berries on the ground, and those in the bushes were still green.

Suddenly he spied a bird feeder hanging from a tree branch. It was filled with berries.

He frowned. "These are fermented," he said.

"What does 'fermented' mean?" inquired Buster.

"It is what happens to fruits like apples and grapes and berries when they get

The boy detective moved carefully among the birds and the berry bushes.

old," answered Encyclopedia. "For instance, fermented apple cider turns to apple wine. Some of the sugar is turned into alcohol, and alcohol can make you drunk."

"Are you saying that someone has put fermented berries in the feeder to get the birds drunk?" asked Sally.

"Whoever it is picks the ripe berries from the bushes and off the ground," said Encyclopedia. "Then he stores them. After they have fermented, he puts them in the feeder."

"And when the birds drop down for a snack, they get drunk, just like a man who drinks too much wine," said Sally. "What a cruel joke!"

"The fermenting berries could be stored in that tool house," said Buster.

"Hey, you kids!" a voice called. "This is my yard. What do you want?"

It was Carl Higgensbottom, one of Bugs Meany's Tigers. He came out the back door of the house.

"We know what you've been doing to the poor birds just for laughs," snapped Sally. "You should be reported to the police."

"This girl has counted too many cows," said Carl.

"Don't be smart," said Sally. "Open the tool house. I'll bet there are fermenting berries in there."

"You ought to be playing with the squirrels," jeered Carl. "Nobody's been in the tool house for six months. But if you must see . . ."

He drew a ring of keys from his pocket and unlocked the tool house.

Inside were a table and three chairs. On the shelf above the open window stood a half-filled glass jug of apple cider, a candle, and several boxes of matches.

"Last year we kept the lawn mower in here," said Carl. "But the roof leaked. Then for a while this spring, us Tigers used it for meetings while we fixed up our clubhouse."

"Encyclopedia," whispered Buster. "There isn't a berry in sight. Maybe we were wrong about Carl."

Carl grinned. "You sure were, but nobody's perfect," he said grandly.

He went into the house and brought out a bag of doughnuts and four paper cups. He passed out the doughnuts and filled the cups with apple cider from the glass jug in the tool house.

"Are you trying to bribe us?" demanded Buster. He sank his teeth into the doughnut and drank the apple cider as if he enjoyed being bribed.

"I don't want any hard feelings," said Carl.

Sally turned to Encyclopedia. "Can't you prove Carl is lying?" she said.

Encyclopedia tasted the doughnut and apple cider. Thoughtfully he licked his lips.

"The proof isn't hard," he said.

WHAT WAS THE PROOF?

(Turn to page 110 for the solution to The Case of the Apple Cider.)

The Case
of the
Two-Dollar Bill

Sumner Finklefooter stepped up to the Brown Detective Agency and bellowed, "Down with one-dollar bills!"

"Gee, Sumner," said Encyclopedia. "What have they ever done to you?"

"Nothing," answered Sumner. "It's what they've done to Thomas Jefferson that makes me sore."

Thomas Jefferson, the third President of the United States, was Sumner's hero. Once, when his father said he'd like to see some change in him, Sumner had swallowed five Jefferson nickels.

"What have one-dollar bills got to do with Jefferson?" asked Encyclopedia.

"They've made him the forgotten

Sumner Finklefooter bellowed, "Down with one-dollar bills!"

man!" said Sumner. "Everybody knows whose picture is on the one-dollar bill— George Washington's. But how many people know who is on the two-dollar bill?"

"Thomas Jefferson," whispered Encyclopedia.

"Aw, you've got too much head," objected Sumner. "Nobody else in town would have known, because there aren't any two-dollar bills around. Everybody uses one-dollar bills. I aim to correct that."

"Are you going to write your Congressman?"

"I'm going to write every Congressman and Senator in Washington, D.C.," said Sumner. "When you have a cause like mine, you can't think small."

"Sumner," said Encyclopedia with admiration. "Jefferson would have been proud of you."

"All I want is more two-dollar bills printed," said Sumner. "What good is one dollar? You can hardly buy anything with it today."

"You're making sense," said Encyclopedia. "I ought to raise my fee—"

"Not yet!" exclaimed Sumner. He laid twenty-five cents beside the boy detective. "I want to hire you. I need to get the names and addresses of all those men in Washington."

Encyclopedia returned Sumner's twenty-five cents.

"No charge," he said. "I was going to the library today anyway. We can look up the names there."

As they biked to the library, Sumner talked about his grand idea. The two-dollar bill would be as common as the one-dollar bill. Thomas Jefferson would soon rest in every cash register, purse, and pair of pants in Idaville!

At the library, Encyclopedia went to the reference desk. He asked for the book *Members of Congress.*

"Joe Munson has it," said Mrs. Silvers, the head librarian. "You may have it when he's through. But it must not be taken from the building."

Joe Munson was sitting at a table by himself, surrounded by books. *Members of Congress* was open in front of him, and he was copying from it

"It's total war!" declared Sumner

under his breath. "Joe is a fan of Ulysses S. Grant. He wants Grant's picture moved from the fifty-dollar bill to the one-dollar bill."

"He's got a tougher fight than you," said Encyclopedia by way of encouragement.

"The dirty rat!" said Sumner. "I told him I was going to you for help. He probably raced straight here. He'll keep that book all afternoon. His letters will get to Washington ahead of mine!"

"You can't do anything but wait," said Encyclopedia.

"Oh, no? I'll fix him," vowed Sumner. "I'll give him the Sumner stare."

Sumner sat down at the table and stared. Joe looked up. He saw Sumner staring at him. He shifted uncomfortably.

Encyclopedia knew Joe couldn't take the famous Sumner eyeballing very long. He would soon give up and leave. Then Sumner would have *Members of Congress*.

In the meantime, there was nothing for Encyclopedia to do. So he went to the shelves marked "New Arrivals—One-Week Books." He had chosen three when Sumner hurried to him.

"Joe hid my two-dollar bill!" Sumner blurted.

"Sssh!" said several grown-ups angrily. "Sssh!"

Encyclopedia pushed Sumner outside where they could talk. Excitedly, Sumner told what had happened.

Joe had asked him for a two-dollar bill. Joe said he wanted to copy the serial number in order to prove to Congress that there were more two-dollar bills in use than fifty-dollar bills.

"I'm too trusting," said Sumner. "I gave him the bill. I should have given him a cracked lip!"

After giving Joe the bill, Sumner had got up to get a drink. The water fountain wasn't working, and so he had walked across the street to the gas station.

When he returned, Joe was gone. The table was empty except for *Members of Congress*, which lay open. Stuck beneath it was a note:

> *Sumner—I put your two-dollar bill between pages 157 and 158 of the gray book. Thanks—Joe.*

Sumner had questioned the library aide, Clyde Jones. Clyde said that after Joe had left, he had cleared the table of books except for *Members of Congress*. He never removed books which were opened till closing time.

Then, Clyde said, he had put the other books on the table into his library truck and returned them to the shelves. He remembered a gray book. But he didn't remember where he had returned it.

"Joe sure got even with me for staring at him," said Sumner. "What a rotten trick he pulled. There must be a thousand gray books in the library—ten thousand, maybe. It'll take days to find my two-dollar bill!"

"Take it easy," said Encyclopedia. "I know where to find it."

HOW DID ENCYCLOPEDIA KNOW?

(Turn to page 111 for the solution to The Case of the Two-Dollar Bill.)

The Case
of the
Ax Handle

Saturday morning Encyclopedia went down to Mill Creek to fish.

He found the gang already there—Pinky Plummer, Herb Stein, Benny Breslin, Fangs Liveright, and Billy and Jody Turner. They looked as if the world had come to an end.

"Just when the fish were biting like crazy, we ran out of worms," moaned Benny Breslin.

"I can find you more," said a boy as he stepped from behind some palm trees. He picked up the can that had held the worms.

"I'm Ambrose Vining. I'll be back," he

said and disappeared as suddenly as he had come.

Encyclopedia and his pals looked at one another and followed at a distance.

Ambrose walked slowly. He stopped often to pick up a branch, which he studied carefully. Each time he either threw it away or kept it instead of the one he had.

Finally he came to some soft, shaded ground. He put down the can and sank to his knees. He pushed the branch into the ground and rubbed it.

"This kid is weird," said Benny Breslin.

"Wait ..." said Herb Stein. "He stopped rubbing."

Worms had wiggled up near the branch. Ambrose dropped them into the can. Then he pushed the branch into another spot and rubbed again.

Encyclopedia and his pals could not hold their curiosity in. They stepped forward from hiding.

"How'd you do that?" demanded Jody Turner. "I mean, what is the trick you do with the branch?"

Ambrose pushed the branch into the ground and rubbed it.

"I fiddle," said Ambrose.

He explained. In the daytime, worms remain in the ground. So the worm hunter fiddles—he pounds a stick into the ground and rubs it to make it tremble.

"I get it," said Encyclopedia. "The trembling spreads through the earth and brings the worms to the surface."

"Does anyone else know about worm fiddling?" asked Billy Turner.

"Lots of people," said Ambrose. "They use different strokes. And different tools. Some use ax handles. Some use sticks of wood or whatever works best for them."

Fangs Liveright stared at the worms wiggling in the can. "How long has this been going on?"

"Since before I was born," answered Ambrose. "But tomorrow is the big day. The first International Worm Fiddling Championship will be held in Glenn City. I'm entered."

The boys gathered around Ambrose. They slapped his back and wished him luck.

Encyclopedia went one better. The

next day he and Sally rode the bus to Glenn City to see Ambrose make history.

A crowd of a thousand was on hand to watch the championship contest on the high school football field. The two detectives spied Ambrose seated under the stands. He was near tears.

"The championship will start in a few minutes," he said. "I don't have anything to fiddle with!"

"Good grief!" exclaimed Sally. "How come?"

"I loaned my best ax handle to Justin Rogers yesterday," said Ambrose. "Justin's mother is in the contest. He said he'd like her to try my ax handle and maybe she'd buy one like it for the championship."

"You were a good sport to lend it," said Sally. "I'm sure you'll get it back in time."

"If Justin doesn't show up, I've had it," said Ambrose. "I'm only a second-rate worm fiddler without my best ax handle."

Suddenly he gasped in relief.

"There's Justin," he said.

A boy of seventeen came hurrying over. He carried Ambrose's ax handle. It was broken in two.

"I don't know what to say," apologized Justin. "I leaned the handle against a box in the garage last night. This morning I forgot about it. I drove the car over it backing out."

"Didn't you hear the crack?" asked Encyclopedia.

"I had the car radio going," said Justin. "I felt the wheels run over something, but I thought it was the garden hose. Honest, Ambrose, it was an accident. I'm sorry."

Ambrose was stunned. He held the two pieces of the handle. The print of a car tire showed clearly at the place where the handle had broken.

A whistle blew. Mr. Pardee, the head judge, was calling the worm fiddlers to the field.

There were forty-nine men and twenty women and Ambrose, representing thirty states and seven foreign countries. Each had a twenty-foot square of field surrounding a stake. Whoever made the most worms come up in his square would be the world champion worm fiddler.

"I'm a loser," groaned Ambrose. "I've got nothing but my two bare hands to make those worms see daylight."

"You're not licked yet," said Encyclopedia. "Use the longer piece of your ax handle. You've got to *try!*"

"I suppose half an ax handle is better than my fingernails," agreed Ambrose. He trudged to his square.

A gun went off. The crowd roared. The First International Worm Fiddling Championship had begun.

Ambrose fiddled as if for his very life. It was soon plain that he was in a nip-and-tuck battle for the lead with Justin's mother.

They fiddled worm for worm till the gun sounded ending the contest. Justin's mother had won with twenty-four worms. Ambrose had fiddled up twenty-three for second place.

"If only you could prove Justin broke

Ambrose's ax handle on purpose, Encyclopedia!" said Sally.

"I can," answered the boy detective.

HOW?

*(Turn to page 112 for the solution to
The Case of the Ax Handle.)*

**Solution
to
*The Case of the Champion Skier***

Mr. Ware, the kidnapped man, was a champion water skier who didn't want anyone to know he was learning to ski on snow.

So he told only two persons—his wife and Harry Smith.

Harry Smith was one of the six friends Mr. Ware invited to his birthday party.

Encyclopedia saw that five of the gifts were in keeping with Mr. Ware's known interest in water skiing.

But Harry Smith had brought a gift useful only for skiing on snow—*ski wax!*

The police arrested him. Having given himself away, he told where Mr. Ware was being held prisoner.

Mr. Ware was freed unharmed.

Solution
to
The Case of Smelly Nellie

Bugs Meany was weak from the smell of ambergris. So he wasn't thinking too clearly when Encyclopedia questioned him.

And he knew nothing about ambergris except what Smelly Nellie had told him—that it was worth five dollars an ounce.

Bugs said his Tigers had found the ambergris on the ocean bottom while skin diving. Then they had rolled the lump near the shore and waited for the tide to go out.

That was the lie that gave him away!

Ambergris doesn't sink to the bottom of the ocean.

As Encyclopedia knew, it is found *floating* on the water.

Bugs returned the ambergris to Smelly Nellie.

**Solution
to
The Case of the Flying Submarine**

Bugs wanted to get even with the boy detective, who always outsmarted him.

So he said that Encyclopedia and Sally tried to open the submarine and steal parts.

Jess backed up his leader—too well.

Jess claimed that Sally had "tripped Bugs," and that Bugs "went down." That is, Bugs fell on the ground which a two-day rain had made muddy.

Thus Bugs's pants should have been muddy. Instead they were clean. The only mud was one speck, which he flicked off.

Encyclopedia told his father to "look at Bugs's pants."

When Chief Brown saw the clean pants, he knew the Tigers were lying.

Solution
to
The Case of the Boy Boxers

When Elmer went to the water fountain, he let in Jim Hill. Jim stole the money from the office.

Jim might have got clean away, but he knocked over the lamp. So Elmer had to throw suspicion off himself.

He therefore told Pete and Oscar that he was going to telephone Encyclopedia for help. When he reached the telephone in the office, he lost his head. He could not dial.

He was wearing boxing gloves!

He got Jim Hill, who had hidden in the closet, to dial Encyclopedia's number for him. Elmer hoped Encyclopedia would overlook the mistake.

But Encyclopedia was not fooled.

Elmer got the money back from Jim and returned it before the Youth Center opened on Monday.

**Solution
to
*The Case of the Model Universe***

Wilford had bought a half-inch model of the earth. Then he had dreamed up Professor Wolfgang Schmidt and the model-universe exhibit.

He had hoped to make himself some fast money by selling shares in the fake idea to the children of the neighborhood.

Unfortunately for Wilford, he knew nothing about the distance between the stars. But Encyclopedia knew.

Wilford's model universe wouldn't fit into the Yankee Stadium or the Grand Canyon.

In fact, it wouldn't fit on earth.

The stars are too far apart. It wouldn't help even if the model universe were built to the scale of an earth no more than half an inch across. The nearest fixed star would still have to be placed twenty thousand miles away!

Solution
to
The Case of the Flower Can

Bret came to Stella's house to find the Confederate half-dollar.

"I hid it in the flower can," she told him.

So he looked in the flower can. That was his slip.

Only the thief who had bumped into her earlier and had seen the coin in the flower can would have known what she meant.

Had Bret been innocent, he would have thought Stella had said: "I hid it in the *flour* can."

Remember, he was holding the can of flour for her.

Bret confessed. Posing as a door-to-door salesman, he had been stealing for some time.

Whenever he rang a doorbell and no one was at home, he'd try the door, and if it was open, he'd sneak into the house and steal something valuable.

Solution
to
The Case of the Half-White Horse

Earle Coughlin, the real thief, had seen Sol riding Half-and-Half on the seaway path and so got the idea of pinning the jewelry robbery on him.

But Earle described only the side of Half-and-Half which he had seen—the side with the black spots and the bell-shaped mark. And he said he could read "Idaville Riding Academy" on the back of Sol's shirt as he dismounted.

Thus, according to Earle's own words, Sol had dismounted on the horse's right side. The horse's left side was all white, remember?

A horseman, however, gets on and off at the horse's left side—*never* the right.

Earle Coughlin was sent to jail for the robbery of Mr. Fairchild's jewelry.

Solution
to
The Case of the Apple Cider

Carl knew there were no berries fermenting in the tool house. He had put them in the feeder that morning.

Then he had swept the floor, and he had opened the window to get rid of the smell of fermenting.

Still, he wanted to show that he was innocent. So he said, "Nobody's been in the tool house for six months."

To win over the children, he gave them doughnuts and a cup of apple cider from the half-filled jug in the tool house. That was his mistake!

Once opened, the apple cider would have fermented and tasted sour after six months. That it still tasted sweet proved Carl had been in the tool house drinking it recently.

Carl promised never to get birds drunk again.

Solution
to
The Case of the Two-Dollar Bill

Joe thought that Encyclopedia would suspect Clyde, the library aide. Clyde could have read the note Joe left for Sumner, and then taken the two-dollar bill from the gray book on the table.

But Encyclopedia knew differently.

He knew Joe had seen Clyde coming around with the library truck while Sumner was away from the table. So Joe had written the note to Sumner.

Then Joe put the two-dollar bill in his pocket and left the library.

He had made one mistake. He wrote that he hid the two-dollar bill between pages 157 and 158—impossible!

You can't put anything between pages 157 and 158 of a book. They are two sides of the same sheet of paper—back-to-back pages!

**Solution
to
*The Case of the Ax Handle***

Justin lied when he said that he had backed the car over the ax handle by accident.

If that were true, both the front and back wheels on one side of the car would have passed over the handle and left tire prints.

But there was the print of just one tire on the handle!

That proved Justin had moved the car only enough to break the handle. After one wheel had passed over the handle, he had stopped and pulled the broken pieces from under the car!

He knew that with Ambrose unable to fiddle at his best, his mother would win the championship.

However, when his mother learned the truth, she awarded her title to Ambrose.

ABOUT THE AUTHOR

Since the publication of the first *Encyclopedia Brown* book in 1963, DONALD J. SOBOL has written roughly one book a year. In 1967, at a Children's Book Fair, he explained, "I began writing children's mysteries because the mystery element was really very small in the so-called mysteries that were written for children and I felt that this was a shame." In 1976, the *Encyclopedia Brown* series was the recipient of a special 1976 Edgar Allan Poe Award, presented by the Mystery Writers of America in recognition of these books as the first mysteries that millions of children read. In addition to the *Encyclopedia Brown* series, Mr. Sobol has authored over twenty books for young readers. A native of New York, he now lives in Florida with his wife and children.